Little Red
Robin

How Bobby
Got His Pet

Do you have all the Little Red Robin books?

- [ ] **Buster's Big Surprise**
- [ ] **The Purple Butterfly**
- [ ] **How Bobby Got His Pet**
- [ ] **We are Super!**
- [ ] **New Friends**
- [ ] **Robo-Robbie**

Also available as ebooks

If you feel ready to read a longer book,
look out for more stories about Bobby

Little Red
Robin

How Bobby
Got His Pet

Jo Simmons
Illustrated by Steve Wells

SCHOLASTIC

Scholastic Children's Books
An imprint of Scholastic Ltd.
Euston House, 24 Eversholt Street
London, NW1 1DB, UK
Registered office: Westfield Road, Southam, Warwickshire, CV47 0RA
SCHOLASTIC and associated logos are trademarks and/or registered
trademarks of Scholastic Inc.

First published in the UK in 2014 by Scholastic Ltd

Text copyright © Jo Simmons, 2014
Illustrations © Steve Wells, 2014

The rights of Jo Simmons and Steve Wells
to be identified as the author and illustrator of
this work have been asserted by them.

ISBN 978 1407 13883 1

A CIP catalogue record for this book is available from the British Library

Printed in China.

1 3 5 7 9 10 8 6 4 2

This is a work of fiction. Names, characters, places, incidents and dialogues are
products of the author's imagination or are used fictitiously. Any resemblance to actual
people, living or dead, events or locales is entirely coincidental.

www.scholastic.co.uk/zone

Bobby Cobbler had wanted a pet ever since he was very small. A dog, perhaps. Or a cat. Even a goldfish would do. But his parents always said one word: No!

I will never have a pet, thought Bobby, sadly.
Luckily, he was wrong.

So what happened? Well, it's a funny story, and it starts on the next page.

TURN OVER

When Bobby was six, he moved to a cottage in the countryside.

Bobby's dad stopped the car outside the cottage. Bobby couldn't wait to get out. "It looks nice," he said. "But I must explore to be sure!"

Bobby ran into the garden and. . .

"Yes!" he shouted.

The garden was huge – big enough for games and adventures – with a field full of cows beyond. It also had a beautiful, tall horse chestnut tree (that's a conker tree, to you and me).

YES!

"This place can't get any better," said Bobby, grinning.

But it could and it did. . .

Soon after the Cobblers moved in, Mrs Upguffy came to visit. Mrs Upguffy owned the farmhouse across the fields. And the cows, too. She had red cheeks, big hands and said "jolly" a lot.

"My cat Pencil has had some jolly little kittens," she said. "Do you fancy coming to see them, Bobby?"

Then she winked at him – WINK!

Bobby was excited. Kittens are cute. Surely his parents would let him have one? Everyone loves kittens, right?

Wrong. Bobby's parents did not love kittens.

"No!" said Bobby's mum, when Bobby asked if he could have one. "You can visit them after school, but that is all."

The next day, Bobby went to see the kittens.
He found them playing in the kitchen.

There were three girls, called simply One, Two and Three.

"Their new owners can name them," explained Mrs Upguffy. "There's no jolly point naming them now."

The fourth kitten was a boy. Mrs Upguffy just called him the Boy. Sometimes even the Bad Boy! Why?

Because this little cat
had a big personality.
When visitors tickled
him, he scratched.

When they walked
away, he jumped on
their legs and climbed
up their trousers!

15

So when Bobby came to see the kittens, he felt nervous. Would the crazy kitten scratch him, too?

Bobby sat down by the basket. One, Two and Three stayed asleep, but the Boy woke up. Two green eyes blinked at him.

Then a kitten head popped up. Then the kitten jumped into Bobby's lap and purred.

"Well!" said Mrs Upguffy when she saw the two of them. "That kitten has scratched everyone else, but he jolly well likes you."

Bobby smiled. He felt pleased and proud. The scratchy cat was not scratching him! *Perhaps we can be friends*, thought Bobby.

Bobby visited the kittens every day after school. The Boy became his favourite. They played, they cuddled, they chased. It was fun!

Until, one day, Bobby tickled the Boy on the
tummy . . . and the Boy scratched him!

"Ouch!" cried
Bobby, feeling
shocked to
his socks.

Bobby wanted to run home and hide. He was hurt and upset. But before Bobby could leave, the kitten settled in his lap again and began to purr.

Maybe he is just telling me where I can touch him, Bobby thought, as he calmed down. *Ears – good. Tummy – bad.*

So Bobby learned about the cat – what he liked and did not like – and the cat learned to trust Bobby. Their friendship grew, like a beautiful mushroom on a log.

Soon, One, Two and Three went to new homes. Only the Boy was left, but he scratched anyone who came to visit. Nobody wanted him – except Bobby.

"That cat loves only you," said Mrs Upguffy. "Let me ask your parents if you can jolly well have him."

Mrs Upguffy spoke to Bobby's dad, but what did he say?

You guessed it…

"No!"

That was not all, though. There was more bad news heading Bobby's way. . .

"We are moving again," said Mr Cobbler the next day at breakfast.

"When?" asked Bobby.

"Today," said his dad. "We are going to a busy town with lots of children for you to play with."

"But I don't want lots of children!" cried Bobby, his cheeks burning. "I want my cat!"

"Come on," said Bobby's dad. "He's only a moggy. Nothing special. You will soon forget him."

"Never!" shouted Bobby, and he ran into the garden.

Bobby wanted to cry, but he also wanted to shout with anger. Instead, he kicked a conker that had fallen from the tree. Then he sat down on a tree stump with a thud. Bobby stayed there for a while, feeling upset.

Then he began picking up conkers and dropping them into his backpack.

"These will remind me of the garden," he muttered, sadly.

By the time he had filled his bag, Mrs Upguffy had arrived.

Mrs Upguffy was carrying a backpack that looked just like Bobby's. She put it down next to his. The Boy was inside.

He jumped on to the grass and chased a conker. Bobby rolled another conker. The cat dashed after it.

"He loves conkers," said Bobby. "That's what I would call him, if he lived with me – Conkers!"

"Call him that anyway," said Mrs Upguffy, smiling kindly. "It's jolly perfect."

"Goodbye, then, Conkers," whispered Bobby, pushing his nose into the cat's black fur. "I will never forget you."

Then Mrs Upguffy popped Conkers into the backpack and left.

"Not fair," sobbed Bobby, as he watched her go.
His eyes were soggy, but through his tears Bobby
could just see Mrs Upguffy turn, smile – and wink.
WINK!

Why did she wink? Bobby wondered, as he swung his backpack on to his shoulder. It felt heavy.

Must be all those conkers I picked up, he thought, as he ran back to the house.

On the drive to his new home, Bobby felt sad. When they arrived at the new house, he still felt sad.

Bobby ran up to his new bedroom and sat on the floor for ages, feeling sad some more – until he heard a scratching sound.

Mice? he thought.

He looked at his backpack. It was wriggling.

Bobby pulled the zip open slowly. Pull, pull, pull.

POP!

Two black ears popped out of the bag. Then two green eyes. Then a whole cat. And not just any cat.

CONKERS!

"How did you get here?" Bobby cried.
But Conkers just purred.

"How did he get here?" Bobby's mum cried, when she saw the cat. She was cross.

"I didn't take him," said Bobby. "I promise! He was in my bag. At least I think this is my bag. Maybe Mrs Upguffy took the wrong bag home? With the wrong conkers in it!"

Conkers tiptoed over to Bobby's mum. She tensed up. Conkers usually scratched, after all. But not today. Instead, he rubbed his cheek on her leg.

"He likes you, Mum," said Bobby. "He wants to be with us. Please let him stay. PLEASE!"

Bobby's mum frowned. Bobby's mum thought.
Bobby's mum scratched her head.
Then she said one word:

It was the best Yes! Bobby had ever heard.
Conkers was his. For good. For ever.

So Bobby got a pet, but to this day, he does not know how Conkers ended up in his backpack. He visited Mrs Upguffy a few months later and asked her.

"No jolly idea," said Mrs Upguffy.

Then she winked.

WINK!